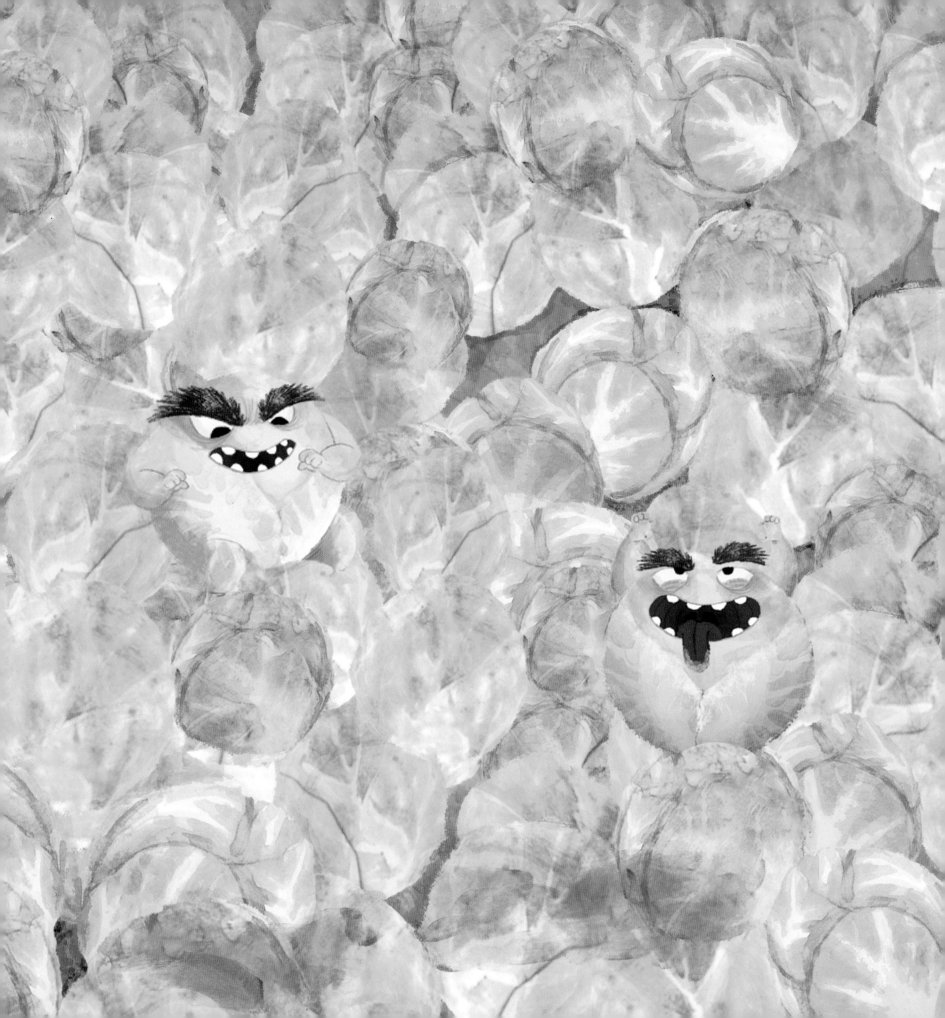

For Cherry and Zora – T.J.

For Oscar & Harry, my very own Sproutlings x - M.B.

First published 2019 by Macmillan Children's Books,
an imprint of Pan Macmillan
The Smithson, 6 Briset Street, London, EC1M 5NR
Associated companies throughout the world
www.panmacmillan.com

ISBN 978-1-5098-9461-1

1 3 5 7 9 8 6 4 2

A CIP catalogue record for this book
is available from the British Library.

Printed in China

The Return of SPROUTZILLA

Written by
TOM JAMIESON

Illustrated by
MIKE BYRNE

MACMILLAN CHILDREN'S BOOKS

It was almost Christmas and Santa and his elves were hard at work. Everything had to be ready because everyone loved Christmas.

Well, nearly everyone! Someone rather large and green
didn't like Christmas one little bit, and he had a plan . . .

In the village of Beamerrie, Jack and Ruby were putting up the decorations. Somehow Dad always managed to get tangled up in the lights. But the one thing missing this year was snow. "You need real snow for snowball fights," grumbled Jack, who had already tried making his own. "Paper is too soft and candy floss is way too sticky!"

Suddenly, there was a knock at the door. It was a group of Santa's little elves. "Jack, Ruby, we need your help again!" they cried in a panic.

"What's up? Where's Santa?" Jack asked.
"Hop in, there's no time to lose!" said one of the elves, as the others jumped back into the sleigh. "We'll explain on the way!"

Jack and Ruby held on tight as the sleigh flew through the air.
"Santa's been kidnapped!" cried one of the elves, "and we think that Sproutzilla
and his sidekicks, Tyrannoparsnip rex and Broccolisaurus are to blame!"

In the North Pole, they searched through Santa's Workshop. "Oh no!" cried Ruby.

An army of Sproutlings whizzed around the room and shot out through the door.

"This can only mean one thing . . . Sproutzilla is back, and he's captured Santa!"

"Quick, to the sleigh!" cried Jack. "We can follow the Sproutlings back to Sproutzilla's lair and rescue Santa!" But Sproutzilla's villainous vegetable sidekicks were watching their every move.

"Are you sure you can drive this thing?" Jack shouted.
"Relax! Tyrannoparsnip rex is miles behind us," yelled Ruby.
"He may be miles BEHIND us, but Broccolisaurus is right in FRONT of us!"

Suddenly the sleigh swerved and jerked. Jack and Ruby tumbled through the sky, straight into Sproutzilla's grasp below.

"Aaaarrrggh!"

Sproutzilla carried Jack and Ruby back to his sproutlair where Santa was already behind bars. Instead of rescuing Santa, now they were locked up alongside him! "If we don't get out of here soon, Christmas will be ruined," Santa warned.

"What a gloomy place! Sproutzilla must be lonely living here," Jack whispered. "Smashing, crashing and ruining Christmas doesn't win you many friends."

That gave Ruby an idea, but for the plan to work she'd need Jack's help. "Finally I get to throw a proper snowball!" Jack cheered.

Just as Sproutzilla opened the door, Jack darted away.

With the green menace out of sight, this was Ruby and Santa's chance to put the plan into action.

Later when Sproutzilla returned to his lair with Jack in his grasp, he couldn't believe his eyes. It looked like Santa's grotto!

"So this was your amazing plan, Ruby?" Jack scoffed. "Christmas decorations?"
"I want to show Sproutzilla the fun and joy of Christmas," Ruby explained.

But Sproutzilla was soon on the rampage again! "I've got a plan!" Jack whispered. "This Christmas it won't just be Dad getting tangled up in the Christmas lights!"

In no time Jack, Ruby and Santa had Sproutzilla bundled up.

Now that they had Sproutzilla's full attention, Ruby explained the true meaning of Christmas. It isn't just about eating yummy food, and giving and receiving presents (though presents are always welcome!), Christmas is about being with the people you love.

And with that Jack, Ruby and Santa gave Sproutzilla a HUGE hug.
Which he thought was . . . not too bad at all!

"It's great that you've taught Sproutzilla about the joy of Christmas," said Santa,
"But we still have one teeny-weeny problem . . . that green menace has wrecked
my workshop! How will we get all the presents finished in time for Christmas day?"

"Let's set up Santa's workshop here," said Ruby. There's plenty of space."
Sproutzilla grinned from ear to ear. What a terrific idea! But could they
really get every last present wrapped and delivered in time?

. . . only with everyone lending a hand, and yes, that means EVERYONE!

"Go, Tyrannoparsnip rex and Broccolisaurus!"

Finally, every last present was delivered, but the reindeer and the vegetables were too tired to pull the sleigh home.

Luckily, Ruby knew a SPROUT-POWERED way to get back home in time for Christmas . . .

"Here we go!" bellowed Santa. "Hold on tight!"

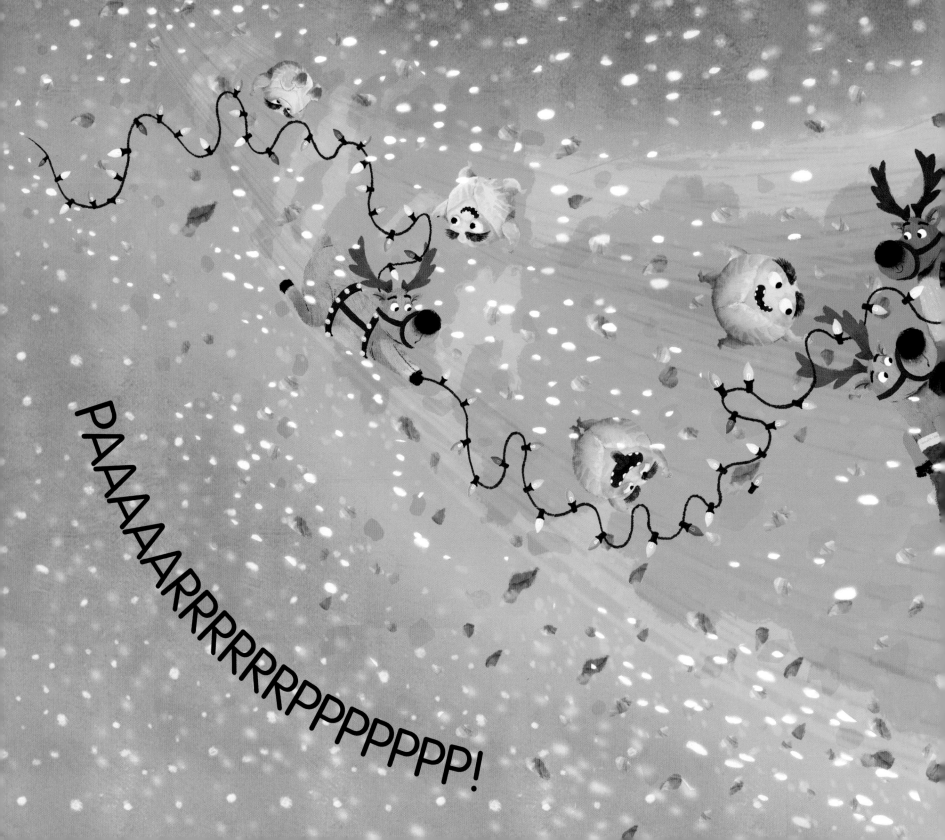

PAAAAARRRRRRPPPPPP!

"I can't thank you enough for saving Christmas!" cheered Santa.

There was just time for one last group hug,
before Jack and Ruby waved goodbye to the sleigh.

But Jack couldn't help noticing there was still no snow! "Look, Jack!" said Ruby, pointing up to the sky. "We might not have snowflakes, but this Christmas we have the next best thing . . . SPROUTFLAKES!"

"Instead of a white Christmas, let's have a green one!"

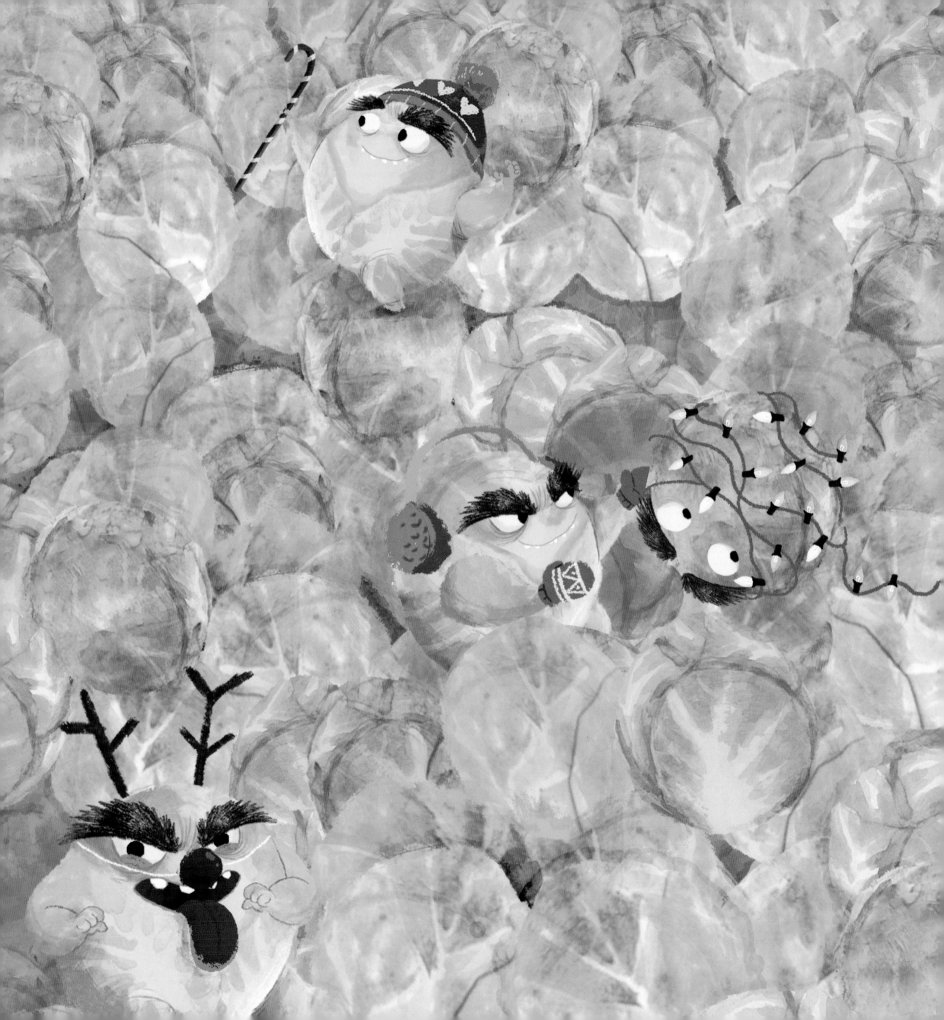